BUZZY BEE
GOES TO SCHOOL

written by Barbara Curie
illustrated by Russell Rigo

© 1983, The STANDARD PUBLISHING Company, Cincinnati, Ohio
Division of STANDEX INTERNATIONAL Corporation. Printed in U.S.A.

The distinctive trade dress of this book is proprietary to Western Publishing Company, Inc., used with permission.

Hi there!
Do you know why I am singing a song?
Well, today as I was just flying along,
I passed the school where some friends of mine go.
And a question arose as I flew to and fro.

I asked myself, "Is there a reason why?
If my friends go to school, why can't I?"
So, tomorrow I am going to school
And I will obey the Golden Rule.

Do you know the Golden Rule? If not, look on the last page of this book. Do you know where the Golden Rule came from? Find Luke 6:31 in your Bible.

I am so happy! I am going to school!
I will obey the Golden Rule.

It is rude to be late. I will hurry on by.
Others may want to be late today; not I.

Oh, my! Oh, my! Is this really school?
Does anyone here know the Golden Rule?

Do you remember the Golden Rule? Can you say it?

Now that is more like it, I would say;
Those children know whom to obey.
I'm going to fly over and sit on that stool.
I want to see what goes on at school.

Titus 3:1 says, "Remind them to be subject to rulers, to authorities, to be obedient, to be ready for every good deed." A person in authority has a right to give rules. Who gives rules at school? Do you obey that person?

Are children all over the world free
To go to school like you—like me?
School is a wonderful place to go;
A place to learn what we need to know.

That boy is cheating to get a good score.
Cheating is wrong in the sight of the Lord.
I wouldn't want someone to copy from me;
So I wouldn't copy from them, you see.

Find 1 Peter 3:11 in your Bible. Read the first sentence of the verse. Try to remember it.

The teacher said each child could pick a book to
 read.
David looked for his favorite, a book on planting
 seed.
But Ben was reading that book, and David got mad;
He started to grab the book, until he saw that Ben
 looked sad.
Then he gave it back to Ben and looked for another
 book.
David felt better, and Ben had a happy look.

Did David obey the Golden Rule? How?

I thought manners were a part of life at school.
I thought children would live by the Golden Rule.
I thought they would be thankful to have some food;
But some of them waste a lot, then act very rude.
Oh, look, there is one boy who knows how to be
   polite;
And I feel very sure that he'll eat every bite.

Amy spelled it wrong and Crystal spelled it right.
Crystal must have studied her words last night.
Friends could help each other learn spelling words
  for school.
That would be a way to obey the Golden Rule.

These children certainly know the Golden Rule.
I'm sure they obey at home as well as here at school.

I am glad I came to school today
And saw the children at work and play.
Some children must learn how to act at school;
But some children do follow the Golden Rule.
The children who seemed most happy today,
Were the ones who tried to follow God's way.

Golden Rule

Do unto others as you would have others do
unto you.